WELLNESS WORKSHOP

BREATHE WITH ART!

ACTIVITIES to MANAGE EMOTIONS

LAUREN KUKLA

Checkerboard Library

An Imprint of Abdo Publishing
abdobooks.com

abdobooks.com

Published by Abdo Publishing, a division of ABDO, PO Box 398166, Minneapolis, Minnesota 55439.
Copyright © 2023 by Abdo Consulting Group, Inc. International copyrights reserved in all countries.
No part of this book may be reproduced in any form without written permission from the publisher.
Checkerboard Library™ is a trademark and logo of Abdo Publishing.

Printed in the United States of America, North Mankato, Minnesota
102022
012023

Design and Production: Mighty Media, Inc.
Editor: Rebecca Amundson
Cover Photographs: Mighty Media, Inc. (project photos); Perfect Angle Images/Shutterstock Images (child)
Interior Photographs: Alena Ozerova/Shutterstock Images, p. 9; Annaartist/Shutterstock Images, p. 29 (wheel); girl-think-position/Shutterstock Images, p. 21; ImageSource/iStockphoto, p. 7; MIAStudio/Shutterstock Images, p. 17; Mighty Media, Inc. (project photos), pp. 14, 18, 22, 26; PRASANNAPiX/iStockphoto, p. 13; QualityStockArts/Shutterstock Images, p. 25; Richard Peterson/Shutterstock Images, p. 5; VALUAVITALY/Shutterstock Images, p. 11; vita_dntk/Shutterstock Images, p. 10 (bag); Vitalliy/Shutterstock Images, 10 (pins)
Design Elements: Huza Studio/Shutterstock Images (illustrations); Mighty Media, Inc.

Library of Congress Control Number: 2022940658

Publisher's Cataloging-in-Publication Data

Names: Kukla, Lauren, author.
Title: Breathe with art! activities to manage emotions / by Lauren Kukla
Description: Minneapolis, Minnesota : Abdo Publishing, 2023 | Series: Wellness workshop | Includes online resources and index.
Identifiers: ISBN 9781532199783 (lib. bdg.) | ISBN 9781098274986 (ebook)
    Subjects: LCSH: Mind and body--Juvenile literature. | Wellness programs--Juvenile literature. | Human emotions--Juvenile literature. | Yogic breathing--Juvenile literature.
Classification: DDC 152.4--dc23

CONTENTS

Wellness Wheel 4

Just Breathe 6

Name That Emotion! 8

Emotions Are... 12

Unmasking Emotions 16

Mindfulness 20

Restorative Nature 24

Wellness Wrap-Up 28

Glossary 30

Online Resources 31

Index 32

WELLNESS WHEEL

What makes you feel good? Healthy food, such as fruits and vegetables? Playing soccer or running in the park? Or maybe laughing at a funny video with your best friend? Wellness is all these things and more. It's the space around you, the way you handle **stress**, and how you find fulfillment and purpose in life.

Psychologists often divide wellness into six to eight **dimensions**, or groups. The dimensions are equally important. They are often shown in a graphic called a Wellness Wheel.

YOU MAKE CHOICES EVERY DAY THAT HELP CONTRIBUTE TO YOUR WELLNESS. THIS BOOK WILL EXPLORE EMOTIONAL WELLNESS AND HOW IT AFFECTS YOUR OVERALL WELL-BEING THROUGH FUN ART PROJECTS AND ACTIVITIES. SO TAKE A DEEP BREATH, AND LET'S GET STARTED!

SOCIAL WELLNESS

has to do with the way you interact with others. This includes relationships with family and friends. It also includes **empathizing** with strangers.

PHYSICAL WELLNESS

includes healthy habits to help your body work its best! This includes eating healthy foods, wearing a seatbelt, exercising, and getting enough sleep.

ENVIRONMENTAL WELLNESS

means understanding the ways in which your environment affects your overall well-being. It also means caring for the world around you.

EMOTIONAL WELLNESS

includes understanding the many emotions you feel every day. It also means accepting and feeling good about who you are and learning to manage **stress**.

SPIRITUAL WELLNESS

means finding a sense of meaning and purpose in life. It includes your values and beliefs.

INTELLECTUAL WELLNESS

means being aware of your creativity and mental abilities. It includes challenging your mind and growing your knowledge.

JUST BREATHE

Have you ever felt happy, excited, sad, angry, or stressed? Or maybe you've felt a physical sensation, like a tightness in your chest before a big test or a fluttering in your stomach while riding a roller coaster. And maybe you weren't sure why you were feeling that way.

We all experience strong emotions. By learning to recognize those you are experiencing, you can learn more about yourself. We can't control the emotions we are feeling, but we can control how we react to them.

EMOTIONAL WELLNESS TIPS

- Learn to recognize and name your emotions without labeling emotions as good or bad.
- Learn to calm strong emotions through breathing or **meditation**.
- Find techniques to help you handle stressful situations.
- Accept and love yourself for who you are right now.
- Develop a support system of caring people you love and trust.

1, 2, 3, BREATHE

Belly breathing is a great way to calm strong emotions. The best part? You can do it anytime and anywhere!

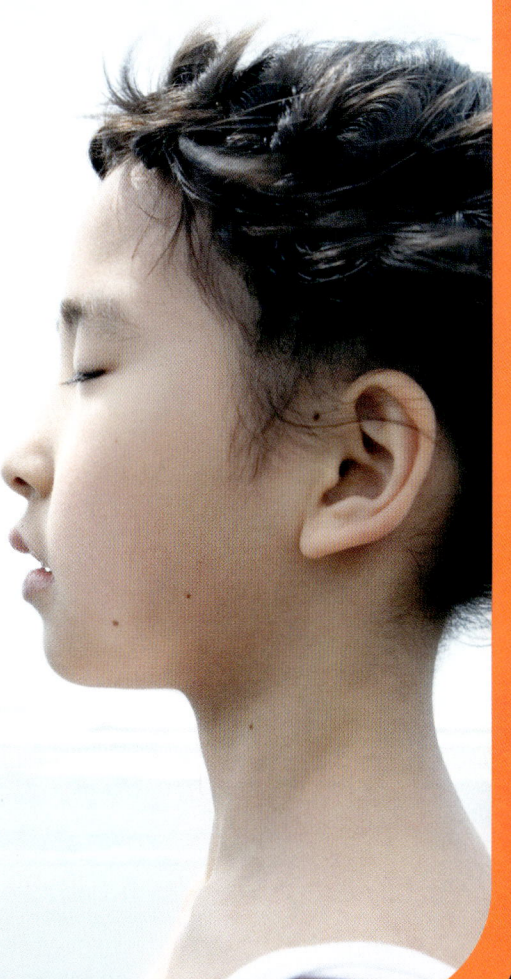

1. Find a spot to sit in a comfortable position. Gently close your eyes.

2. Take a slow, deep breath through your nose. Silently count to three as you **inhale**. As you feel your belly expand, imagine you are filling it up like a balloon.

3. Slowly breathe out through your mouth. Silently count to three as you **exhale**. Imagine the air is whooshing out of your belly balloon, taking some of the strong emotion you are feeling with it.

NAME THAT EMOTION!

Emotions are the way you feel about something happening to you. Humans experience many emotions. These can change by the hour or even by the minute! You might feel sad after an argument with a friend, then learn that your grandma is coming for a visit and feel excited. You may even experience opposite emotions at the same time! We can't control the emotions we feel, but we can try to control how we respond to them.

The first step to coping with strong emotions is to recognize and name the different emotions you feel. Take a few minutes to think about the emotions you experienced over the last few days. Write these emotions on a piece of paper. Don't judge yourself or the emotions. Just write!

You can write your list of emotions in a journal and update or add to it any time you'd like.

EMOJI PINS

Turn the emotions list you made on page 8 into emoji pins!

WHAT YOU NEED

- Pennies
- Paint & paintbrushes
- Permanent markers or paint pens
- Clear glue
- Hot glue gun & glue sticks
- Pin backs

WHAT YOU DO

1. Paint each penny. Let them dry.

2. Use permanent markers or paint pens to decorate each penny. On each, draw a face representing one of the emotions from the list you made on page 8.

3. Cover each penny with clear glue to give it a glossy look. Let the glue dry.

4. Use hot glue to attach a pin back to each penny.

WELLNESS IN ACTION

Attach your pins to a backpack, jacket, or other clothing item you wear or see often. When you start experiencing a strong emotion, catch yourself before you react to it. Then follow these steps: Find the pin that best represents the emotion you are feeling. State "I am feeling _____." Take a deep breath. Then decide how you want to react.

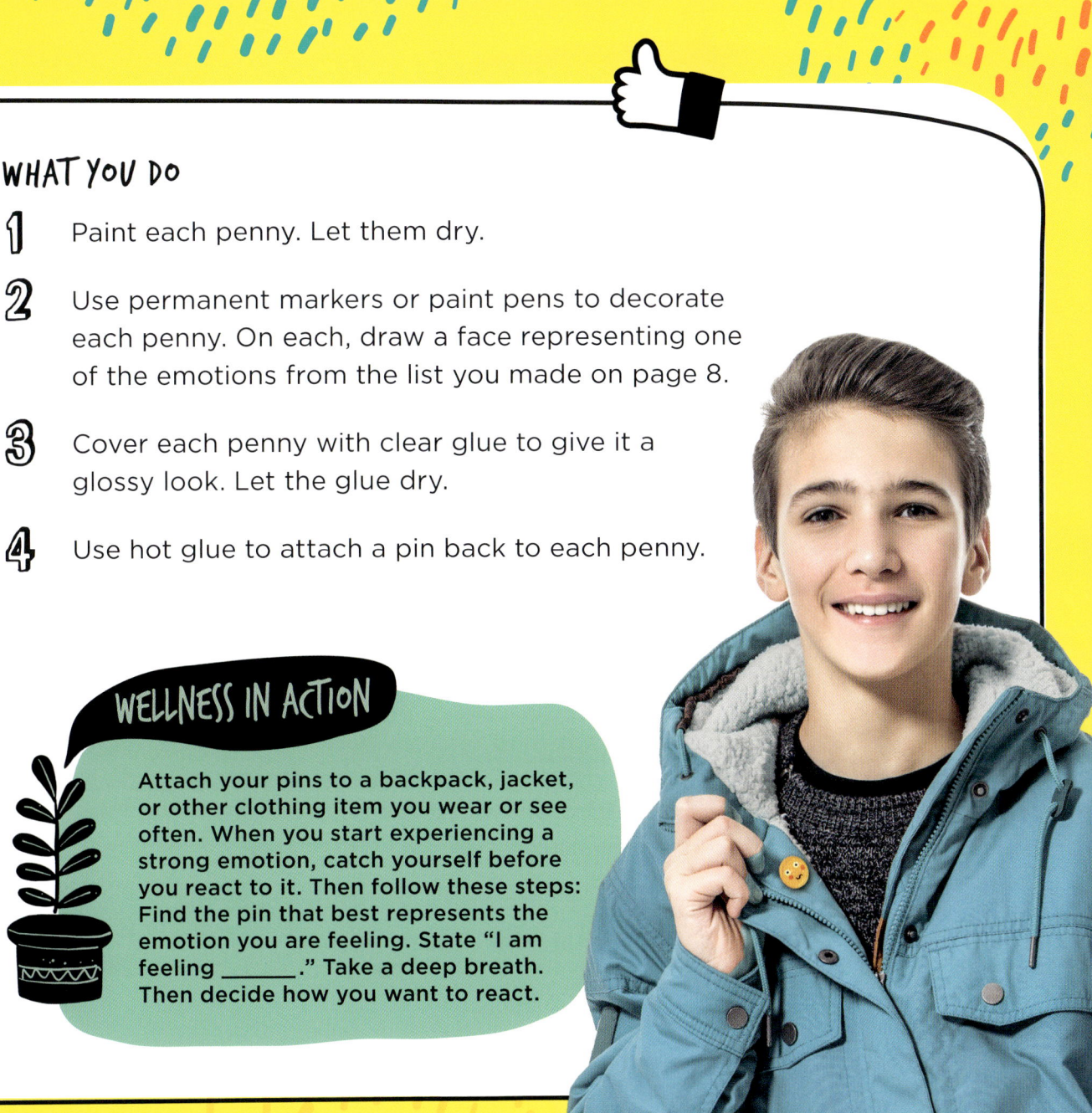

EMOTIONS ARE . . .

Emotions are important tools. They give us information about how we are feeling as things happen to us. Some emotions, like joy, can be pleasant. Others, like anger, can be unpleasant. But all emotions are equally important. Each one helps us understand our reactions to the environment around us. Emotions aren't good or bad. They just are.

It can be helpful to think of emotions like colors. There are no good or bad colors. But we might find some colors more pleasing than others. Some people think colors can **trigger** certain emotions. Greens and blues can be calming. Red and orange can energize you. And purple can spark a burst of creativity!

In India, people throw colored powders on one another to celebrate a festival called Holi. Each color has a special meaning.

COLOR THAT EMOTION

Glitter jars are common relaxation tools. Many people find that watching the glitter swirl and settle has a calming effect. Make a rainbow of glitter jars in colors that can help you connect with certain emotions.

WHAT YOU NEED

- Measuring cup
- Clear glitter glue
- Mixing bowl & spoon
- Hot water
- Funnel
- Clean, clear spice jars
- Ruler
- Fine glitter in various colors that represent different emotions to you
- Food coloring
- Decorative materials, such as paint or stickers

WHAT YOU DO

1. Pour ¼ cup glitter glue into a bowl. Add 1 cup hot water and stir until the mixture is smooth.

2. Use a funnel to pour the mixture into a spice jar, filling the jar up to about 1 inch (2.5 cm) from the top.

3. Add one color of glitter to the mixture. Put the cap on the jar and shake to mix it well. Start with a little bit of glitter and add more as needed.

4. Uncap the jar. Add a few drops of food coloring that is the same color as the glitter. Cap the jar and shake it well.

5. Decorate the lid of the jar to represent the emotion connected to the color you chose.

6. Repeat steps 2 through 5 to make more glitter jars. Repeat step 1 to make more glue mixture if needed.

WELLNESS IN ACTION

Use your jars to help you channel certain emotions. Maybe you are working on a school project and feeling stuck. Take whatever jar represents creativity to you and flip it upside down. Watch the glitter slowly swirl and settle. Let go of any emotions, focusing only on the glitter's movement. How do you feel?

UNMASKING EMOTIONS

People sometimes handle difficult emotions, such as sadness, by acting them out. This might mean lashing out at a friend or sibling when they do something that hurts you. Other people try to handle difficult emotions by **suppressing** them. Suppressing emotions is not healthy. But neither is reacting to your feelings by taking them out on others.

Anger, sadness, and other unpleasant emotions are natural. They are part of being human. It's important to recognize and accept these emotions as they come, without passing judgment on them. But it's also important to not let your emotions control you.

By unmasking your emotions, you allow yourself to fully experience them. Then you can better handle your response to them.

Recognizing your emotions is the first step to handling them in a healthy way.

EMOTION MASK

Difficult emotions are a part of life. Practice allowing yourself to fully experience these emotions by creating a mask representing an emotion you find challenging.

WHAT YOU NEED

- Balloon
- Newspaper
- Ruler
- Measuring cup
- White glue
- Water
- Mixing bowl & spoon
- Roll of duct tape
- Pushpin or sharp object
- Craft knife or scissors
- Elastic cording
- Paint & paintbrushes

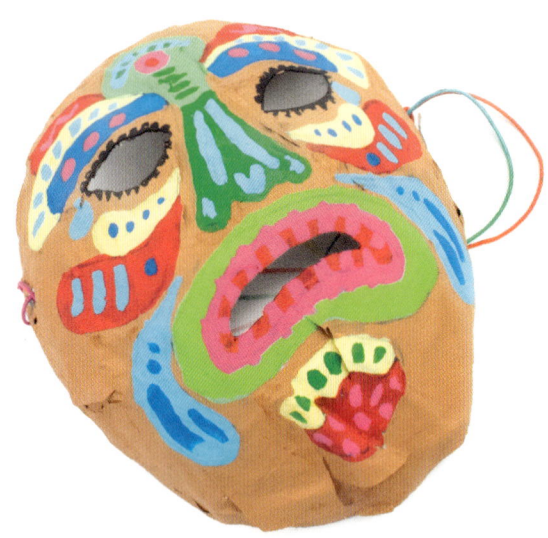

WHAT YOU DO

1. Inflate a balloon. Tear newspaper into strips about 1 inch (2.5 cm) wide.

2. Mix 1 cup glue and ½ cup water in a mixing bowl.

3. Submerge a newspaper strip in the mixture. Grab one end of the strip with your fingers and hold it over the bowl. Use two fingers on the other hand to sandwich and **squeegee** excess glue off the strip. Lay the strip on the balloon.

4. Repeat step 3 until half of the balloon is covered with about 15 layers of strips. Set the uncovered side of the balloon on a duct tape roll and allow the strips to fully dry.

5. Use a pushpin or sharp object to pop the balloon, leaving the newspaper form behind. Cut the form into a mask shape. Cut holes for the eyes and mouth.

6. Poke a hole on either side of the mask near the edge. Cut a length of elastic cord a bit wider than the mask. Thread and knot one end of it through each punched hole.

7. Decorate the mask to represent the difficult emotion you chose.

WELLNESS IN ACTION

When you aren't feeling any big emotions, put on your mask and think of a time when you experienced its emotion. How did you respond then? Do you wish you had behaved differently? Act out how you would like to respond to the emotion.

MINDFULNESS

When people talk about emotional wellness, the term *mindfulness* often comes up. But what does it mean? Mindfulness is full awareness of what is going on in the present moment.

What is happening in your environment? Let your senses guide you. What do you see, hear, smell, and feel? Do you feel tightness in your body, or are you relaxed? Finally, what emotions are you experiencing? Do any specific thoughts keep popping up?

The key to mindfulness is to notice how you are feeling without passing judgment on it. No feelings are good or bad. But simply by being aware of what you are experiencing, you can improve your emotional well-being!

Meditation is a practice many people do to improve their mindfulness.

21

MANDALA MEDITATION

Mandalas are symbols important to Buddhist and Hindu spiritual traditions. A mandala is a design that repeats from its center. While slowly making or coloring the mandala, the creator lets their mind slip into a **meditative** state.

WHAT YOU NEED

- Paper
- Pencil
- Large bowl or plate
- Small bowl or plate
- Drinking glass
- Ruler
- Crayons, markers, or colored pencils

WHAT YOU DO

1. Trace around a large bowl or plate on a piece of paper. Find and mark the exact center of the circle.

2. Use a ruler to draw four lines through the center, dividing the circle into eight equal parts.

3. Center a small bowl or plate in the circle and trace around the object.

4. Center a glass in the circle. Trace the rim. You should now have three circles of different sizes and 24 different sections.

5. Begin drawing a design in a section closest to the circle's center point. Create an identical design in the section next to it. Repeat until the first circle is filled in.

6. Repeat step 5 with the second circle, and then the third. Then color your mandala!

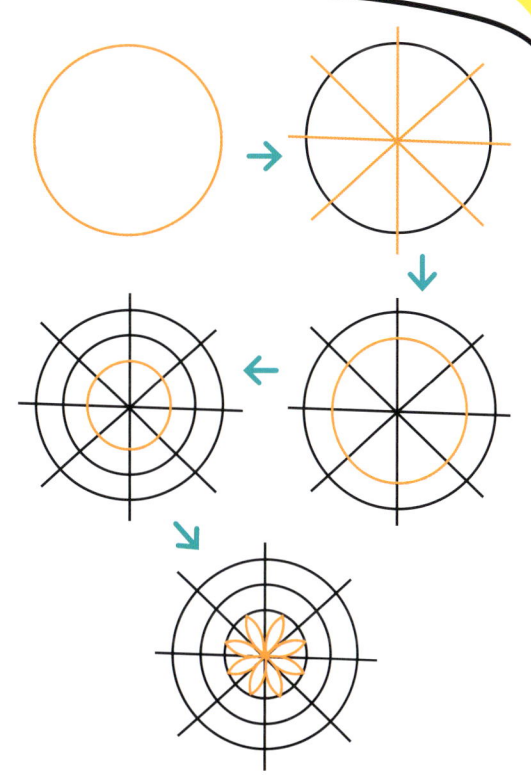

WELLNESS IN ACTION

Art can be very healing. Whenever you are feeling **stressed** or upset, channel your emotions into an art project, such as a mandala. As you create, slow your breathing, and let your mind relax.

RESTORATIVE NATURE

Have you ever felt refreshed after a walk in the woods? For many people, spending time in nature is healing. People have looked to nature to improve their overall well-being for thousands of years.

In the 1980s, many people in Japan adopted a practice called forest bathing. A forest bath is a slow, mindful walk in the woods. The goal isn't to travel far. A person may walk only a few hundred feet during a forest bath. The goal is to **immerse** yourself in the natural world, focusing on its sights, sounds, and smells.

If you can't go to a forest, spending time near any type of nature can help your well-being. Sit in a park and listen to the birds. Stop near a garden and smell the roses. Enjoy the soft **hues** of winter sunrise or the brilliant colors of a rainbow.

Scientific studies have shown that spending time in nature can increase pleasant emotions.

BITTY BONSAI

You may not be able to grow a forest to bathe in. But caring for a tiny tree can connect you to the natural world! Bonsai are trees trained to grow in small containers. The art of growing bonsai began in China thousands of years ago. Today, people grow bonsai all over the world.

WHAT YOU NEED

- Small tree or shrub
- Ruler
- Scissors or garden pruners
- Wire in various thicknesses
- Shallow pot or dish with 2 to 4 drainage holes
- Soil
- Rocks (optional)
- Water & fertilizer (to care for your tree)

BONSAI BASICS

Almost any tree can be a bonsai tree. But certain trees and shrubs are the best candidates for bonsai beginners. These trees and shrubs include juniper, ficus, and Chinese elm.

WHAT YOU DO

1. Obtain a small tree from a nursery or get permission to dig one up that is growing outside. The tree should be less than 1 foot (0.3 m) tall.

2. Use a scissors or garden **pruners** to trim the tree's **canopy** until it resembles a miniature adult tree. You can remove up to one-third of the tree's **foliage** without harming its growth.

3. Wrap the trunk in medium-thick wire. Wrap larger branches in a thinner wire that you connect to the main trunk.

4. If the tree is planted, remove it from its planter. Untangle the roots and remove any soil. Prune up to one-third of the roots' length.

5. Cover the bottom of the pot with soil. Place the tree in the pot and cover its roots with more soil. Lay rocks around the tree if you'd like.

6. Bend the wire branches in a way that pleases you.

7. Provide your bonsai with plenty of sunlight, and water it about once a week or anytime the soil is dry. Fertilize the bonsai according to the fertilizer's instructions. Prune the branches a few times a year to keep your bonsai's shape.

WELLNESS IN ACTION

Make caring for your bonsai a weekly mindful ritual. As you water your tree, take in its scent. Listen to water splashing onto the soil. Relax and be amazed by the wonders of nature.

WELLNESS WRAP-UP

Wellness isn't about making a major healthy decision once or twice. It's the many little choices you make every day. Some choices, such as naming your emotions, may be easier than others, such as controlling your response to those emotions.

Emotional wellness is just one part of your wellness journey! Learn about more wellness **dimensions** by reading the other books in this series. Their activities and projects can help you flex your mindfulness muscles and improve your well-being. But you get to decide what wellness looks like for you.

Follow the steps on page 29 to make your own Wellness Wheel like the one on page 5. Let the wheel help guide the choices you make at home, in school, and with friends and family. And always remember to slow down and breathe.

MY WELLNESS WHEEL

WHAT YOU NEED

- Plate or bowl
- Card stock
- Pencil
- Ruler
- Crayons, markers, or colored pencils
- Scissors

WHAT YOU DO

1. Trace the rim of a plate or bowl on a sheet of card stock.

2. Find and mark the exact center of the circle.

3. Use the ruler to draw three lines through the center point, dividing the circle into six equal sections.

4. Label each section with a wellness **dimension**: Emotional, Environmental, Intellectual, Physical, Social, and Spiritual.

5. In each section, draw a picture showing what that dimension means to you.

6. Cut out the circle. Hang it somewhere you will see it every day!

29

GLOSSARY

canopy—the uppermost spreading, branchy layer of a tree.

dimension—one of the elements making up a complete unit.

empathize—to show understanding of another person's feelings.

exhale—to breathe out.

foliage—the leaves of one or more plants, especially growing leaves.

hue—a color or a shade of a color.

immerse—to plunge or dip something into a fluid so that it is completely covered.

inhale—to breathe in.

meditation—the act of thinking deeply and quietly. Something related to meditation is meditative.

prune—to cut away or remove what is extra or unwanted. Pruners are tools used to prune plants.

psychologist—a person who studies the science of the mind and behavior.

squeegee—to smooth and wipe a surface by spreading, pushing, or wiping liquid material on, across, or off it.

stress—a physical, chemical, or emotional factor that causes bodily or mental strain. Things that cause this strain are called stressful.

suppress—to force down or back.

trigger—to activate or cause a strong, and usually negative, emotional reaction in someone.

ONLINE RESOURCES

To learn more about activities to manage emotions, please visit **abdobooklinks.com** or scan this QR code. These links are routinely monitored and updated to provide the most current information available.

INDEX

bonsai, 26, 27
bonsai project, 26, 27
breathing, 4, 6, 7, 11, 23, 28

China, 26
colors and emotions, 12, 14, 15

emoji pin project, 10, 11
emotion mask project, 18, 19
exercise, 4, 5

food, 4, 5, 28
forest bathing, 24, 26

glitter jars project, 14, 15

Japan, 24

mandala project, 22, 23
mandalas, 22, 23
meditation, 6, 22
mental abilities, 5
mindfulness, 20, 24, 27, 28

nature, 24, 26, 27

psychologists, 4

relationships, 4, 5, 6, 8, 16, 28

sleep, 5
stress, 4, 5, 6, 23

values, 5

wellness dimensions, 4, 5, 28, 29
Wellness Wheel, 4, 5, 28, 29
Wellness Wheel project, 29